Willisk's Tooth

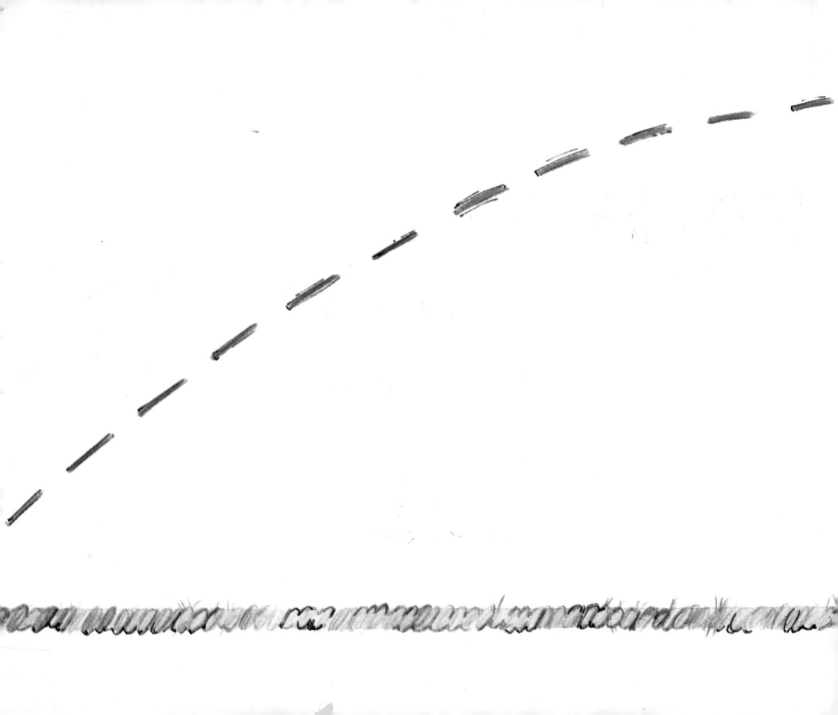

Willisk's Tooth

ANDREW MARTYR

illustrated by
PAULA LAWFORD

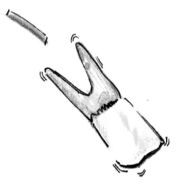

PICTURE CORGI BOOKS

Also by Andrew Martyr and Paula Lawford, and published by
Picture Corgi Books:
WINSTON'S ICE CREAM CAPER

WILLISK'S TOOTH
A PICTURE CORGI BOOK 0 552 524948

Originally published in Great Britain by Hamish Hamilton
Children's Books

Hamish Hamilton edition published 1985
Picture Corgi edition published 1989
Text copyright © 1985 by Andrew Martyr
Illustrations copyright 1985 © by Paula Lawford

Picture Corgi Books are published by Transworld Publishers
Ltd., 61-63 Uxbridge Road, Ealing, London W5 5SA, in Australia
by Transworld Publishers (Australia) Pty. Ltd., 15-23 Helles
Avenue, Moorebank, NSW 2170, and in New Zealand by
Transworld Publishers (N.Z.) Ltd., Cnr. Moselle and
Waipareira Avenues, Henderson, Auckland.

Made and printed in Portugal by Printer Portugesa

Willisk the Walrus was very unhappy.
He had terrible toothache.

So had everyone else who was waiting to see the dentist.

Soon the nurse called Willisk in.
"It's your turn," she said.

Doctor Cavity, the dentist, was waiting for Willisk.

Doctor Cavity looked into Willisk's mouth. "Open wide," he said,

"wider . . . wider . . . wider. Ah, now I see it. You have a bad tooth."

Suddenly Willisk sneezed, A-ɑ-ɑ-tish-o-o-o!

. . . and he became firmly stuck in the chair. Doctor Cavity and the nurse could not pull him out.

In despair, Doctor Cavity telephoned for help.

Soon two policemen arrived.

They covered Willisk with slippery soap.
But he stayed firmly stuck in the chair.

Then the fire brigade arrived.
They squirted water over everybody.

Poor Willisk was soaked, but he remained firmly stuck in the chair.

Then the ambulancemen arrived.

They tied a rope around Willisk . . .

. . . and asked everyone to pull on it.

And so, the policemen pulled.

The ambulancemen pulled.

The firemen pulled.

All the other patients pulled. Even Doctor Cavity and the nurse pulled.

Suddenly – POP! – Willisk shot out of the chair. Everyone flew through the air.

They ended up in a huge pile on the floor. Willisk landed right on top of them . . .

. . . closely followed by his bad tooth.

Willisk's toothache had completely gone, and at last he was very happy!

Here are some other Picture Corgis you may enjoy:—

MR BILL AND THE FLYING FISH
by Georgie Adams, illustrated by Margaret
Chamberlain

MR BILL AND THE RUNAWAY SAUSAGES
by Georgie Adams, illustrated by Margaret
Chamberlain

ARTHUR'S TOOTH
by Marc Brown

BUT MARTIN!
by June Counsel

THE TROUBLE WITH JACK
by Shirley Hughes

WINSTON'S ICE CREAM CAPER
by Andrew Martyr and Paula Lawford

PLANET OF THE MONSTERS
by Stephen May

THE SILLY SILLY GHOST
by H. E. Todd, illustrated by Val Biro